Christmas, 2007

Carol, Bill and Jesse,

Wishing you a Christmas
filled with happy holiday
memories.

love,
Tim, Patty & Michaela

THE
LITTLEST COWBOY'S
Christmas

THE LITTLEST COWBOY'S *Christmas*

BY MICHAEL CHANDLER
ILLUSTRATED BY TERRY JACOBSEN

PELICAN PUBLISHING COMPANY
GRETNA 2006

The word "Pelican" and the depiction of a pelican are trademarks of Pelican Publishing Company, Inc., and are registered in the U.S. Patent and Trademark Office.

Library of Congress Cataloging-in-Publication Data

Chandler, Michael.
  The littlest cowboy's Christmas / By Michael Chandler ; illustrated by Terry Jacobsen.
      p. cm.
  Summary: "The author retells here for young children the story of when his family was invited to a cowboy's barn to celebrate Christmas Eve. As the cowboy's horse enjoyed a carrot and oats pie, another guest hummed 'Silent Night.'"—Provided by publisher.
    ISBN-13: 978-1-58980-381-7 (hardcover : alk. paper)
  1. Denver, John—Anecdotes—Juvenile literature. 2. Singers—Anecdotes—Juvenile literature. 3. Christmas Anecdotes—Juvenile literature. I. Jacobsen, Terry, ill. II. Title.

  ML3930.D42C5 2006
  782.42164092—dc22

                                                2006010528

"Silent Night, Holy Night" recording and selection courtesy of The RCA Music Group, a unit of SONY BMG Music Entertainment.℗1975 BMG Music.

Printed in China
Published by Pelican Publishing Company, Inc.
1000 Burmaster Street, Gretna, Louisiana 70053

THE LITTLEST COWBOY'S CHRISTMAS

You remember one Christmas most of all. Maybe it was a gift you once received. Maybe it was a surprise visit from an old friend. You've enjoyed many, but this one was different.

Tonight, as we sit among friends and neighbors, I'll share mine.

Many years ago, my wife, Jackie, and I lived on
a small horse ranch in Little Woody Creek, just
outside Aspen, Colorado.

My son, Preston, now with a wife and two beautiful little girls of his own, was only four. My daughter, Melissa, wasn't yet born.

During the winters, we'd hook up a snowplow to the front of our farm tractor. I'd bundle up Preston, plop him on my lap, and the two of us would chug up and down Little Woody pushing snow this way and that. We did this not because we had to, but because the two of us would feel so good on those freezing winter days, snuggled together, giggling, singing, and shoving snow around.

We felt important, tackling all those drifts, blazing trails, passing livestock with their flared nostrils throwing shafts of steam like medieval dragons, and coming home to Jackie hours later with rosy cheeks and tall tales.

During one early December, Little Woody Creek received several feet of fresh snow. Preston and I brewed up our hot cocoa, climbed onto our tractor's steel seat, and chugged up some untracked, snow-choked road.

We didn't know where it went—only that it was waiting for us, and our tractor. At the end stood a snowbound home with an old green Jeep parked outside.

As our tractor pushed this way and that, and our laughter cut the crystallized air, a rugged-looking cowboy came out of the house.

He walked up to us and asked, "Did somebody hire you to do this?"

"Nope."

"Then why are you doing it?" he asked.

" 'Cause it's fun!" we replied.

A wide smile crept onto the stranger's face. He stretched out his hand to shake mine. And I shook hands with one of the five best friends I've ever had in my life.

"The name's Joe," he said. "Joe Henry." He had jet-black hair and a mustache, a chiseled face, and well-worn jeans topped off with a faded work shirt. He looked as if he'd just come off a six-week cattle drive. He didn't look tired—far from it. He looked alive and vibrant, and very rugged.

Joe was a quiet sort. He never bragged; he was very different. I would find out over the years that Joe is singularly driven to fulfill his own destiny, regardless of what others think of his reasons. He is a solitary man, nearly always alone, but never lonely.

Preston and I asked what he was doing in this snowbound house. "Writing songs," Joe said. "And books. And cowboy poetry."

Joe had been a miner and a boxer and a hockey player and a steamship sailor and a ditch digger and a real live buckaroo. We found out that his Appaloosa stud, Lefty, was stabled in an old barn just up the road from our own home.

Christmas was coming. As it approached, Joe walked up to our house one day. He asked if Preston and I would like to come up to the barn Christmas Eve and help him celebrate the season with his horse, Lefty.

Joe said that he was making Lefty a Christmas carrot and oats pie and that another friend was bringing his boy too, about Preston's age. He said the other fella was a country boy and could play a guitar some, and we could all sing a carol or two.

So Christmas Eve arrived, and Preston and I went.

The barn wasn't more than a quarter-mile from our house, so with a kiss from my wife, Jackie, the two of us donned our winter coats and walked up there in the moonlight, the frozen snow crunching beneath the soles of our boots.

Joe greeted us the moment we reached the barn, sliding a stall door open so we could enter.

This barn was a working barn. There was no concrete, no steel, no insulation, no electricity, no offices—just sweet hay covering the dirt floor, a loft filled with the summer's harvest, wooden pens, and high ceilings crisscrossed by rough-sawn rafters.

In the center, Joe had arranged a half-dozen hay bales to sit on. Next to them stood a small evergreen tree. It had candles perched on its boughs, popcorn strings, and a tin-foil star that Joe had made. One present rested beneath: Lefty's Christmas carrot and oats pie.

The fella with the guitar was there. He rose to greet Preston and me. His son, no bigger than my own boy, stood at his side. The fella warmly introduced himself, but he didn't have to. Though we'd never met, I recognized him immediately.

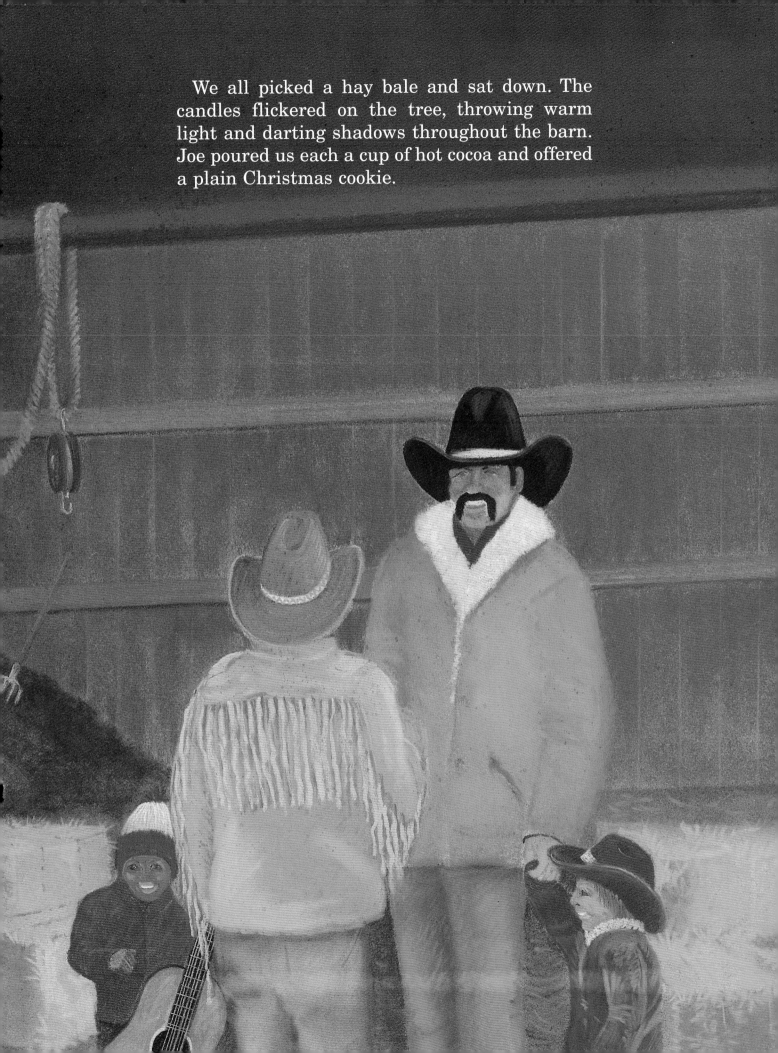

We all picked a hay bale and sat down. The candles flickered on the tree, throwing warm light and darting shadows throughout the barn. Joe poured us each a cup of hot cocoa and offered a plain Christmas cookie.

Lefty peered from his stall, his shaggy head
hanging over the gate, his huge dark eyes watching
us. I felt as if the stallion knew why we were there,
and what Christmas Eve meant.

As we toasted Lefty, as we toasted each other, the fella with the guitar began to play. We all sang "Jingle Bells" and "Deck the Halls" and "Frosty the Snowman." We all laughed, we all hooted, we all forgot most of the second verses. Counting the livestock, just six of us experienced something I had never felt before: true peace . . . boundless joy . . . utter humility . . . friendship . . . and the meaning of Christmas.

Finally, Joe got up and walked over to the tree, bending down to carefully pick up Lefty's pie. As he turned and walked to the stall, the fella with the guitar began to softly hum "Silent Night." Joe offered the pie to Lefty, and the horse began to eat.

The barn was filled with only two sounds:
Lefty's slow and muffled crunch of those crisp
carrots, and the guitar fella's soft humming of
"Silent Night."

I felt as if I were in heaven. We all did. Lefty finished about the same time as the song, and we all stood there with glistening eyes and deep personal thoughts.

We looked at each other, and Joe spoke. "Merry Christmas" was all he said.

We all shook hands and said goodbye.

Preston and I reopened the barn door, waved, and began our return walk home under a sky full of a trillion shining stars, each one brighter than the next. We didn't say anything as we walked hand in tiny hand. We both knew that what had happened was very special, very important—maybe even more than pushing snow around with our little tractor.

When we got to the front door of our home, Preston looked up at me, tugging at my sleeve. "Who was the man with the guitar, Daddy?"

Though known throughout the world by millions of people who adored him, his music, the Country Roads and Rocky Mountain Highs of his voice, it wasn't important that I mention his last name. "It's John, Preston. The guitar fella's name is John."

That night, he and his young son were just another couple of cowboys, sharing Christmas Eve with a few friends, and an Appaloosa horse named Lefty.